A CASE MOST CHRISTMAS

CONNOR WHITELEY

No part of this book may be reproduced in any form or by any electronic or mechanical means. Including information storage, and retrieval systems, without written permission from the author except for the use of brief quotations in a book review.

This book is NOT legal, professional, medical, financial or any type of official advice.

Any questions about the book, rights licensing, or to contact the author, please email connorwhiteley@connorwhiteley.net

Copyright © 2024 CONNOR WHITELEY

All rights reserved.

DEDICATION
Thank you to all my readers without you I couldn't do what I love.

CHAPTER 1
22nd December 2023
Canterbury, England
12:05

Private Eye Bettie English had always loved how amazing, wonderful and brilliant the Canterbury Christmas Markets were as she went along the long cobblestone high street, with the huge red, black and green brick and glass buildings that made up the high street were covered in tinsel and great decorations that really made Bettie love the holiday season.

There were immense crowds of old and young, large and small, tall and short people in all sorts of great-looking jeans, black overcoats and cream coats as they went around the little market stalls hoping to find their next great Christmas present.

Bettie was really glad she had already gotten all of her presents sorted except one or two but she wasn't that worried. Bettie was walking behind two elderly people who were shuffling along in their heavy black coats and Bettie really wished they would hurry up but she was just enjoying the atmosphere.

The sweet aromas of mulled wine, brandy and caramel filled the icy cold Friday afternoon air that made the taste of Christmas form on her tongue, and Bettie was so excited about the big day coming up.

Loud music was playing over the stalls and the delightful singing of carollers made Bettie's heart fill with Christmas cheer and she really did love the markets. Everyone was just so happy, cheerful and everyone was having such a great time.

And it was Christmas when Canterbury really became alive and Bettie loved every single moment of it.

"Mummy," a little boy said.

Bettie smiled down at her pram as her little two angels Harrison and Elizabeth were looking at all the pretty lights, sounds and waving randomly at strangers as they went past.

Bettie's sister Phryne was walking next to her in a very long black overcoat, black trousers and white blouse. She didn't know why her sister looked so formal compared to Bettie's jeans, black hoody and leather jacket but she was just glad to have her sister back.

It had been ages since Phryne had come out of therapy that helped her deal with all the anger and rage she had about her ex-husband leaving her with a kid she never wanted and Bettie couldn't deny, her sister had been a bitch to her wonderful nephew Sean and his boyfriend but Phryne seemed to be better now.

And Bettie was slightly willing to let Phryne back into their lives and she really hoped she wasn't going to regret it.

"Mummy," Elizabeth said.

"Yes beautifuls," Bettie said.

"Look!" Harrison shouted as he pointed into the crowds but she had no idea what he wanted. "It's Santa!"

Bettie laughed as a very large red Santa drifted through the crowd on the back of someone because it was a decoration and not the real thing.

"We'll go and see the real Santa later," Bettie said.

Harrison's bottom lip twitched. "Not all Santas are real?"

Bettie laughed when something else made a noise and that thankfully distracted the kids long enough for Bettie to pop forward the little rain cover so the kids might forget about the question.

They were only 15 months old and Bettie loved them more than anything else in the entire world. And she was so looking forward to seeing the look on their faces when she gave them their presents on Christmas day morning.

Bettie's phone buzzed and Bettie pulled over inside the doorway of a closed shop and answered a video call from her nephew Sean who should be about to fly back from a three-week holiday to

Australia that they had done to see some university friends.

"Hi auntie," Sean said, his tasteful and stylish pink highlights in his blond hair blowing slightly from the air-conditioning on the plane.

"Hi Sean," Bettie said, "Are you due to take off?"

"Any moment now. We'll land early tomorrow morning and then we can spend Christmas together. We look forward to it,"

Bettie smiled as Sean moved the phone slightly so she could see a very burnt Harry was already sleeping on the plane.

"See you soon," Sean said as Bettie heard an announcement from the pilot.

Bettie said she loved him and she ended the call and looked at Phryne. "Are you coming for Christmas?"

Her sister looked shocked at the question. "You would allow me after everything I've said and done?"

Bettie wasn't going to lie and say that she was thrilled about her sister shouting, berating and bullying her own child and Bettie herself for years. And she was a nasty drunk but she felt like Phryne had changed so she was willing to give her a fresh start.

But before Bettie could say anything a firm hand grabbed her shoulder.

Bettie swung around but stopped when she saw the very friendly and frowning face of Agent Daniels, MI5 wearing a very black trench coat, business suit and black shoes.

Bettie instantly knew things weren't good and she was sure she wasn't going to see any more of the market today.

"Miss English," Daniels said, "we have a situation. There's going to be a terror event in the next few hours that would ground every single plane all over the world and grind the world to a halt,"

Bettie smiled as the very idea of that sort of high stakes case excited her a lot more than she ever wanted to admit.

But she already knew that the stakes couldn't be higher because if planes were grounded then that meant Sean and Harry wouldn't be flying home for Christmas.

CHAPTER 2
22nd December 2023
London, England
12:30

Former Detective Graham Adams sat in the back of a black SUV with two MI5 officers next to him wearing black business suits, black shoes and the worst aftershave he had ever smelt. He wasn't sure if it was a cross-between a dead cat or a dead chicken but he hated it all the same.

He had been cooking Bettie, Phryne and the kids a little surprise lunch of crispy roast potatoes, juicy pulled pork and incredible steaks that just melted like butter when the two MI5 officers had turned up wanting to take him to London.

Graham had to admit the great views of London were perfect and beautiful. They were driving right next to the swirling, twirling, churning River Thames with the Shard and other important London landmarks in the distance.

He had no idea where they were but the little brick houses were dirty, rundown and Graham knew this neighbourhood was poor as anything. It was strange to be taken down here but Graham had worked with beautiful Bettie and Daniels way too many times to know that this probably wasn't a normal neighbourhood.

Graham focused on the two MI5 officers as they both readjusted themselves and he coughed on the choking strength of their aftershave. He hated it and he so badly wanted to see the woman he loved.

Bettie always smelt amazing.

He wasn't sure what MI5 could possibly want with him, besides the fact that together him and Bettie were unstoppable but it was what the officers said about the world grinding to a halt.

Graham had heard a lot about EuroControl in recent years because it was a place in Brussels, Belgium that controlled all of European airspace. Whenever a plane wanted to take off they needed to contact EuroControl so they could plan and make sure everything all over the continent was okay and the space at the destination airport was all sorted out too by the time they would arrive.

It was immensely complex but as Bettie had explained it to him, if EuroControl failed then every single plane across Europe would have to be grounded.

The Officers hadn't mentioned that was what was going on but Graham knew it was unfortunately very likely. He just wished the damn officers would tell him more but maybe they didn't know and maybe that was why him and Bettie were needed.

"When we arrive," one of the officers said, "Director Porter will need to talk with you and Miss English about security clearance and more,"

"What's going on?" Graham asked.

The Officers shrugged. "We better tell him," one said to the other.

The Officer to Graham's right frowned. "Yesterday the Home Office received an emergency request for the European Union for the UK to allow Europol agents to investigate a cyber group threatening to hack and cripple EuroControl,"

"Let me guess the Home Office denied the request," Graham said.

The two officers nodded and then they continued. "Exactly, the Home Office said, I quote, *We left you idiots so fuck out and stick your European tongues back up to the Evil Institutions you run,*"

Graham shook his head. That was such an English response.

"But now," an officer said, "we have another problem because MI5 picked up the same chatter so the EU and Europe isn't allowed to investigate it and they don't want to share their intel. So we have a few hours before the cyberattack is launched from UK soil and grinds European airspace to a halt,"

Graham couldn't believe that was happening, but it made sense. The government was trying to act tough on the EU because of the General Election next year and they clearly didn't understand that if a cyberattack was launched from the UK then EU-UK relations would be dead in the water.

But Graham supposed the UK government wouldn't mind that.

"What do you need me and Bettie for?" Graham asked.

The officers frowned. "We have absolutely no idea what to do now. We have no leads, no witnesses, no nothing,"

Graham was surprised when the two officers both looked at him and he could tell they were actually concerned.

"Please Mr Adams I haven't seen my sister in four years and she has nephews I have never met. I want to see them this Christmas," one of them said.

"And my mother's returning to the UK for the first time in a decade. I want to, I need to see her. Please help us,"

Graham nodded. There was absolutely nothing else he would rather do than help out innocent people, solve crime and stop a major cyberattack from destroying so many people's Christmases.

Whoever these attackers were they were monsters and Graham fully intended to make them pay.

But he had to stop them first.

CHAPTER 3
22nd December 2023
London, England
13:00

Bettie was seriously impressed as she stood in the middle of a massive black room with its raven black walls filled with tens upon tens of large TV screens showing events happening all over the world as well as internal memos. Like Bettie's personal favourite the dinner options for tonight.

In the very centre of the room was a huge raised platform, Bettie presumed someone important stood there talking to everyone and trying to rally everyone together. And the rich smell of fruit cake, brandy and mulled wine made Bettie so pleased that even intelligence officers seemed to take part in Christmas celebrations.

There were even little pieces of blue, red and golden tinsel on the edges of the TV screens and Bettie was seriously excited for what was about to happen, and she was more than pleased that MI5 had wanted to her to help.

And to make sure her precious nephew got home in time for Christmas, she was going to do whatever it took, legal or not.

Bettie smiled as a very tall young intelligence officer went past her and sat at one of the massively long rings of computers, desks and comfortable black desk chairs that looped around the raised platform. That really got Bettie interested.

It was clear that this department was understaffed but Bettie supposed that was just a reflection of the British intelligence community at the moment. She wasn't pleased how some of her private eyes had been poached by the Service to deal with things they should be doing but the Service paid well and Bettie didn't mind too much.

As long as her members and the Federation was paid well and protected she didn't really care.

A few moments later Bettie felt two strong arms wrap around her and Bettie kissed Graham's soft beautiful lips. He was so hot, sexy and she felt so much better now that he was there by her side. Exactly where he was meant to be.

Bettie felt her stomach churn a little as a small shot of guilt went through her at Graham no longer being a cop. She hated how it was her investigations, her bending of the rules and her ruthless quest for justice that had given the Cabal behind his suspension and later resignation, an opening and an opportunity to get rid of the man she loved.

She knew that Graham was putting on a front but she so badly wanted to help him go back to being an amazing cop. She just needed to figure out how.

Bettie kissed Graham's soft wonderful lips and she had handed over Harrison and Elizabeth to Phryne earlier who had promised to take them to their mother's for the day, and Bettie had to admit Phryne was a lifesaver.

"Hello," Fran said.

Bettie grinned and hugged her best friend and assistant Fran as a small group of MI5 officers walked in behind her.

Bettie wasn't sure what was happening but given how MI5 had decided to bring in her entire team minus Sean and Harry, she just knew this was beyond serious. And something had to be going on besides the threat from the EuroControl attack.

"Madame President," an elderly man said.

Bettie smiled as MI5 Director Porter came over to her in a large black suit, Christmas tie and brown boots that didn't go with the rest of the outfit, but Bettie really liked Porter. He was a good man, actually cared about the UK and he was a very good talker.

He led her and Graham and Fran over to the huge raised platform as all the intelligence officers took their seats. Bettie tried to focus on them but they all looked so similar with their Christmas jumpers, trousers and white shirts.

"Thank you President English," Porter said, "for

coming at such short notice but we are in crisis mode because we've hit a political problem,"

"Shocker," Bettie said.

Porter laughed. "As you know the Security Services aren't allowed to look into political matters under the Law unless the UK Government approves it. The problem in this case is EuroControl depends on a lot of UK-EU relations,"

Bettie smiled. She could see where the problem was.

"Let me guess," she said, "you have just had an hour-long conversation with the Home Secretary and Prime Minister with them concluding this is a waste of *British* resources,"

"Got it in one,"

Bettie hated that she knew how the current UK Government operated. "What's officially happening because I take it this is a black site?"

Bettie held Graham's hand loosely as Porter nodded.

"You are currently two storeys under London and you are correct. The UK Government doesn't know we're investigating and I will deal with the fallout but I will be damned if I let some cyberterrorists launch an attack from my country without trying to stop them first,"

Fran stepped forward. "Your men said this has the power to make the world grind to a halt. How?"

Bettie looked at Porter for permission to answer which he gave with a small nod. "EuroControl controls every single plane and object that enters European airspace including the UK's. Nothing in Europe can take off or land without EuroControl okaying it first of all. Got that?"

Fran nodded.

"That also means that nothing coming into Europe from the US and Asia and Australia for example, cannot land without EuroControl okaying it,"

"Shit," Graham said. "That also means charity supplies, weapon shipments, supplies to Ukraine and more can't happen. This could cause humanitarian aid to Africa and Ukraine to be delayed and worse,"

Bettie nodded. "I hadn't thought of that but it's true,"

"And," Fran said, "if planes in the US and beyond cannot take off because EuroControl hasn't okayed it. Then US airports will be clogged up and all those airports systems will crumble,"

"Even worse," Graham said, "if Sean's plane enters European airspace and the attacks happen meaning they have no way to land,"

"Fuck," Bettie said. "Then the plane would either have to make an emergency landing along with hundreds of other planes. Or whilst the plane's waiting to land it might run out of fuel,"

"And crash," Fran said.

Bettie looked at Graham and she held her stomach as it churned and flipped. The nephew she loved was in danger and that meant Bettie had to do every single thing she could to catch the bastards threatening to do this.

Bettie looked at Porter. "Tell me everything. Now!"

CHAPTER 4
22nd December 2023
London, England
13:10

Graham forced himself not to be sick as he realised that the nephew he had come to love so much was going to probably die unless they figured out what was happening and who was behind it.

Graham watched as the intelligence officers sitting behind the huge circular rows of computers, desks and desk chairs all spoke to each other about their own panicked family members. And Graham realised that this was a hand-selected group of officers, a very large one, to help them on the case.

He was almost surprised that the department wasn't allowed to investigate this but this was the UK Government after all. Graham knew exactly how dirty they played.

As Porter looked like he was going to get a thick paper folder that a woman was bringing him now,

Graham couldn't deny he really loved the tinsel on the TV screens. It was cosy and it really helped to make the place feel like Christmas and it gave the place a sense of hope.

Something Graham was really, really relying on right now.

"Here," Porter said. "We learnt about the chatter from a far-right forum dedicated to the Destruction of the EU and everything it contains. The forum is mostly just sad sods talking about cats and other far-right crap. But there was one quote that alerted us,"

Porter gave the folder to Bettie and Graham looked over her shoulder.

"EuroControl will control nothing after tonight as the Powers of Three strike to kill them all from the home of the Greatest Empire in History," Bettie said reading from the report.

Graham wasn't sure if the British Empire was that great really but this didn't seem the time for a history lesson.

"What else have you done?" Fran asked.

Porter frowned. "We tried to track the person who made the comments and everyone else in the group, but they all use VPNs so we can't track them,"

"What else?" Graham asked.

He noticed a few intelligent officers smile at their boss.

"I only got the team together an hour ago and then this second message popped up," Porter said taking the file from Bettie. "At 9 pm tonight the

Powers of Three will show the EU that their corruption, Nazism and bids to erase White Power will fail once and for all,"

Graham hated these idiots. They clearly didn't understand how the EU worked but that misunderstanding could easily be blamed on the Government in all fairness.

"What's the Powers of Three?" Bettie asked.

Porter shrugged.

"Is that why you need us?" Graham asked.

Bettie went over to Porter. "What's happening?"

Porter looked at all three of them. "My job is hanging by a thread. Since the world got even more divided after Brexit, COVID and the war in Ukraine, MI5 just hasn't had access to the same information as it used it. I don't have the international reach that the Federation does and I'm scared... I'm scared I'm going to fail,"

Graham looked at the woman he loved and smiled at her. He had always been proud of the Federation and their deals with international intelligence agencies and police forces so the Federation had access to more databases than Graham knew existed.

"You won't fail. We won't fail," Graham said and Bettie kissed him on the cheek.

"Fran," Bettie said turning her to assistant. "Contact the Federation and connect your laptop into their systems,"

"Already done," Fran said plugging her laptop

into the MI5 systems so the Federation databases appeared on some of the TV screens.

"Run the name of that group," Graham said.

A few moments later three alerts appeared in connection to The Powers Of Three, it seemed to be a terrorist organisation, a very small one, that was solely dedicated to the death of the EU and any politician that served in the European Parliament.

Graham noticed how two of the mentions were connected to assassinations of politicians but the last one was a lot more interesting.

It was a security memo sent out by the Polish *Foreign Intelligence Agency* when their leader Frank Clarke gave a speech in October 2021 about Polexit and the memo referred to how the FIA believed there was a creditable threat to several politicians within Poland because of Frank's speeches stirring up hate and demanding political violence.

"Where's Frank now?" Graham asked.

Fran gasped. "Dead two days ago in Rochester, Kent,"

Graham smiled a little. It was a shame he was dead but at least his lies couldn't be spread around anymore, but he couldn't understand why someone would want to kill him.

Graham had worked in Rochester before and around the time of the Brexit referendum, Rochester wouldn't have been opposed to Frank Clarke's ideals and beliefs.

"What does the investigation say so far?" Bettie

asked.

"Cold case for now until the forensic results come back," Fran said. "No leads, no witnesses and no camera footage because they were disabled remotely,"

Graham understood that. If a hacking or terror group was planning to attack EuroControl he couldn't see why some silly cameras would be a problem.

"But if the same people that want to hack EuroControl hacked the cameras," Bettie said, "then why kill their leader Frank Clarke?"

Porter stepped forward. "What if Clarke isn't the leader anymore?"

"And if he isn't then who is?" Graham asked. "And the real question is, is the new leader less or more extreme than the last one?"

A chill ran down Graham's spine as he realised he really didn't want to know the answer to that question because whatever it was it still meant Sean's life was in the balance.

Graham had to see Forensic Specialist Zoey Quill immediately.

A CASE MOST CHRISTMAS

CHAPTER 5
22nd December 2023
London, England
13:30

As much as Bettie loved watching Graham's ass as he went with a small group of MI5 officers to talk to Zoey Quill, and she was so jealous of him getting to talk to her best friend, she couldn't deny how excited she was about the case.

It had everything she loved about being a private eye. High stakes, helping to save innocent lives and it was always great when international crime played a role.

This was going to be great fun.

And at least with Graham not here she could force herself not to feel so guilty over him no longer being a cop, something she still had no idea how to fix.

"Well I regret everything I ever said about your little hobby," Phryne said.

Bettie looked at her sister as she walked in and her and Director Parker hugged like they were best friends and Bettie had absolutely no idea what the hell was going on here.

"Excuse me? You two know each other?" Bettie asked.

"Not at first," Phryne said. "The old fat bastard banged into my car, we got talking and a week later I found out this was all part of some operation,"

Bettie just smiled. That was exactly the sort of man Parker was and she really admired him for it.

"I was simply checking out if you were a friend or foe to the Service and if Bettie was in good hands," Parker said.

Bettie didn't want to argue because Phryne had never ever looked after her or even looked out for her when they were adults or kids. But she was really glad to see her sister.

"Christmas is for family after all Bet," Phryne said.

Bettie gestured her sister should join her on the raised platform.

"I wanted your sister here," Parker said, "to support you and I know her legal firm does criminal cases on the Continent. She might be able to help us,"

Bettie shook her head and grinned. Parker really was a deceitful man, she knew that the Federation already had access (or could easily hack) Phryne's legal files through less-than-legal means so the idea that Parker wanted her here for the files was a lie.

Bettie didn't know how she was guessing that Parker had heard about the family troubles of the past year and he wanted to help fix all the bridges. Something Bettie was open to but not exactly thrilled about, especially as Parker was forcing her to fix them.

"Let's get started," Bettie said. "Phryne what do you know about the Powers of Three?"

Phryne shrugged. "No clue but the officers in the car did fill me in. One legal case that might help you is the trial of Carter Taylor in Germany a year ago,"

Bettie nodded to one of the officers behind his computer and a moment later the case file appeared on the TV screens.

She read it and the guy was a dick. He was arrested protesting outside the German Parliament denying the Holocaust happened, which was a massive crime in Germany. He was convicted but he was killed a week later in prison.

And on the photos of the corpse there was a tattoo of three fists joined together by a Nazi symbol.

"Is that their logo?" Phryne asked.

"Run that symbol through all known databases?" Bettie said to Fran and the MI5 officers.

Fran was the first to stand up and make search results appear on the TV screens. "This is a website dedicated to the creation of the Powers of Three Political party. It didn't come up on any original searches because the name of the political party is in Old English,"

"A little weird for neo-Nazis to use Old English," Phryne said.

Bettie couldn't disagree. "Is there an address or something?"

"You can't be serious," Phryne said. "Are people that stupid?"

Bettie smiled as Fran nodded and pulled up the London address for the headquarters and then a group of MI5 officers pulled up the banking records for the party.

"At least they aren't well funded," Parker said.

Bettie frowned. "If they aren't well funded then how are they meant to pull off the cyberattack?"

"Shit," Parker said.

As small panicked voices filled the room, Bettie couldn't deny that this was bad. The lack of funding sort of proved that the Powers of Three couldn't be behind the cyberattack because they wouldn't have the ability to pay their hackers "good" money, they wouldn't have the money to buy the computer equipment needed and more.

The party just didn't have the resources to pull off an attack like this.

"Unless they know who is and this is a joint venture," Bettie said. "And I bet as soon as we start talking to their new leader whoever they are then we might get answers,"

Parker went silent.

"What's wrong?" Bettie asked.

Parker frowned. "This is an officially recognised

Political Party that holds five council seats across the country, it is registered with the Electoral Commission and I just told you the security services cannot investigate politicians without Government Consent,"

"For fuck sake," Bettie said grabbing Phryne and walking out. "I'll interview the bastards myself but I am saving my nephew no matter what,"

CHAPTER 6
22nd December 2023
London, England
13:55

Graham flat out couldn't believe how lucky he was that Zoey Quill was up in London with her husband and two little angelic children to do some Christmas shopping, see the lights and have a great day. He knew she was absolutely crazy for daring to come up to London so close to Christmas, the queues would be dire and it would be impossible to move.

That didn't stop her though.

Graham hugged Zoey as they met on a very quiet side street and they ducked inside a little black-bricked alleyway as lots of young people went past holding tote bags from companies he was surprised they could afford, long brown and blond hair blew in the wind and some older people even smiled at Graham as they noticed Zoey and him together.

The dark alley might have smelt of mulled wine,

mouldy Christmas cake and urine but Graham was just glad to be somewhere private where they could talk about the case without being overheard and that way Zoey hopefully wouldn't be reported.

As much as he didn't want other people to think they were having an affair or something this really wasn't the time.

He had to admit Zoey looked amazing as always with her long black coat, black trousers and Graham could have sworn she was actually wearing her long white lab coat underneath. He had no idea why but at least it was officially confirmed that she never took it off.

"Sorry to bother you," Graham said. "I know you've been looking forward to this for ages,"

"Nonsense Graham. My husband wanted to sit down for hot chocolate anyway and I don't get to see you enough now you aren't a cop,"

Graham forced a smile. He hated not being a cop but it was his decision and he was never going back to the police. He had always wanted to challenge sexism, racism and homophobia in the police but if they weren't going to support him then he was done with them.

"We all miss you Graham and we understand," Zoey said knowing how much he hated this, "and that's why I'm glad I don't work with the police directly,"

Graham appreciated it, she really was a great friend. "What are the findings from the Frank Clarke murder? Have you got anything?"

Zoey bit her lip. "I really shouldn't be talking about this Graham. This is official police business,"

Graham just looked at her. "Since when does that matter?"

Zoey rolled her eyes. "Fine, lab results won't be done before Christmas but I did find something interesting and we better get walking. I'm getting cold,"

Graham laughed and the two of them glided into the stream of foot traffic that smelt amazing of earthy, flowery and spicy aftershaves that all combined perfectly to create the best smell Graham had ever smelt before.

"Frank Clarke was stabbed once in the neck. It's a very hard angle to achieve so I believe the killer wasn't new at all and the weapon was sharp, double-edged and made from military-grade steel,"

Graham was impressed if they were just the earlier results then he would have loved to know what the complete results would be like.

"Frank Clarke was also dying. I found stage 4 lung cancer that had spread to the brain,"

Graham stopped dead in his tracks and a bunch of people smashed into him so Zoey took him to one side and Graham hissed as the icy coldness of a shop window burnt inside his back.

Graham hadn't expected to hear about lung cancer so soon after the death of his mum, he really missed her and he realised that this was going to be the first Christmas without her.

"I'm sorry I was stupid for not thinking," Zoey said knowing how much he loved his mum. "I don't have to continue if you don't want me to,"

Graham shook his head and focused. "I'm okay for now. Just tell me because we have to solve this case before Sean's life is put at risk,"

Zoey nodded and they both started walking back into the crowd. "So why kill a dying man that probably had four months at best?"

Graham moved out the way of a lamp post and he couldn't deny that was a great question. It made no sense to kill someone that wouldn't be a problem for much longer anyway.

"The only other thing I found was there was female reproductive fluid on his attachment," Zoey said.

Graham laughed at her trying to be subtle about that sort of stuff in public.

"I'll get Bettie to give permission for you to send it to a Federation contractor and hopefully they could get a DNA match by tonight,"

"I'll contact my lab," Zoey said taking out her phone.

Graham was about to cross the street when Zoey hugged him.

"Are you okay?" she asked.

Graham wasn't sure if he was or not. His mum had been so horrible, so evil and so cruel to him over the decades and she had been beyond awful to Sean for being gay and Bettie for daring to be a woman in a position of power.

But she had been so nice in the last two months of her life, and it was that mum that he missed more than anything.

"I'll be fine thanks," Graham said.

"I'm always here for you," Zoey said as Graham crossed the road and he fully intended to take her up on her offer.

But first he had to meet up with Bettie and find out who the hell wanted Frank Clarke dead.

CHAPTER 7
22nd December 2023
London, England
14:00

Of all the places Bettie had never ever wanted to hear Christmas songs, it was certainly in the headquarters of Nazis. As she went through the cracked reinforced glass door into the large single room of the shop-like buildings, she was surprised to see Nazi flags and posters hanging on the sterile white walls, the lights were flickering and the three black desks in front of her were awful.

The entire place stunk of mulled wine, oranges and cranberry that left the taste of Christmas cake form on her tongue and Bettie really didn't like this place. Not one bit.

Bettie looked at Phryne and she forced herself not to laugh at how scared she looked. "I'll protect you sis,"

Phryne gave her a weak nod but Bettie

understood the fear. She seriously didn't want to be in this place any longer than needed.

A moment later a door opened in the back wall and a very tall man walked out wearing a full Nazi uniform and Bettie really wanted to punch the man. He was foul, awful and an insult to what so many innocent men and women died to save the world from.

She didn't know what she was going to be doing to him but he was going to suffer for his stupidity.

"Good afternoon ladies. Are you ready to continue the work of our founder?" the man asked as he sat down at the desk.

Bettie shook her head and showed him her Private Eye ID.

"Oh," the man said. "We are an official political party that is registered and we are entitled to our beliefs,"

"And what are these *beliefs?*" Bettie asked.

"That everyone should be ruled by strong white men and women should focus on the production of white children. Also all these liberal laws about equalities, racism and all that other shit needs to be repealed so we can protect and provide a future for our white children,"

Bettie wanted to be sick. That was twisted.

"Under UK law," Phryne said smiling, "those beliefs might be perfectly legal but they are immoral and if you act on those beliefs then that is when you will be committing crimes,"

"What are you? A lawyer?" the man asked.

"Yes," Phryne said.

The man seemed really stunned. "A woman lawyer? What is the world coming to,"

"Anyway," Bettie said just wanting to get the hell out of here, "you are the political party behind the terror organisation known as the Powers of Three,"

The man's face dropped. "No. I run the political party because I truly believe that overtime we will convince the UK public that Nazism isn't as bad as everyone believes and then we will rise to power peacefully,"

"I will never allow that," Bettie said by accident but she meant every word.

"But my brother and sister," the man said, "they run the para-military side of things that I do *not* have contact with anymore. I don't like them. They are military and they are filled with hate,"

Bettie smiled. "And you aren't?"

The man stood up and frowned. "I only hate little women that do not know their place in society under strong white men,"

Bettie got right in his face. "Challenge me to a fight and I'll prove how strong women are,"

The man frowned and after a moment he sat back down.

"Who is your brother and sister?" Phryne asked.

"Frank Clarke but he's dead as you know," the man said, "and my sister Claire Bailey is MIA. I've tried to contact her, I've tried to contact our friends and I've even contacted her boyfriend who runs our Council operations,"

Bettie still couldn't believe these damn people actually had elected officials.

"I couldn't get a hold of any of them," the man said.

Bettie handed him her business card. "If you hear from them please contact me,"

The man ripped up the business card and Bettie took Phryne right out of there.

As they started walking along a dirty London street with little closed shops on the road to their right and the dirty little council houses filled with sun-bleached tinsel around the windows, Bettie took out her phone and texted Fran to monitor the building's calls and what the man did next.

"I don't think that's a problem," Phryne said subtly gesturing to their left.

Bettie smiled as she spotted a very rusty black car parked on the road and she knew that two MI5 officers were already staking out the place.

"So I take it we don't believe the political party are involved?" Phryne asked.

"Correct," Bettie said. "We have to find the sister and see what she knows but I bet she's going to be the one behind all this,"

"You were incredible in there," Phryne said when they got to the car.

Bettie was a little shocked. Her sister had never praised her before about her job, and as Bettie got in the car, she couldn't help but wonder that maybe her sister had changed for the better.

And maybe she wasn't the foul, awful, rageful sister she had been a few months ago.

Bettie hoped beyond hope she was right.

CHAPTER 8
22nd December 2023
London, England
14:45

Graham, sexy Bettie, Phryne and Fran sat inside a little cosy local café on the outskirts of London. Apparently Phryne had gone back to the secret MI5 lair to check up on something. He wasn't sure he liked the café's small size, there were only four round rusty tables in the whole place with red fabric chairs that he was sure would collapse at any moment but it was great to see Bettie again.

The curtain rails that lined the top of the café were covered in purple, gold and red tinsel that made the café look almost posh and normal. Graham wasn't sure on the wreath that hung on the doors because he was fairly sure something was running around inside them and making a very nice nest for itself.

He had no idea why Bettie wanted to meet here

of all places but he trusted her, he loved her and he was more than willing to follow her to the ends of the Earth. So he picked up a greasy plastic menu and tried to look for something that wouldn't kill him.

There wasn't exactly a lot of choice in that department.

Then he noticed Bettie and Fran had raised their menus to cover their lips and make sure no one could see what they were talking about, or the fact that they were talking at all.

Graham did the same.

"Why are we here?" Graham asked noticing they were the only people in the café.

"Because," Fran said, "I was doing some research in Claire Bailey who had a different father to Frank Clarke and the father works here as a chef,"

"He can't be very good," Graham said.

Bettie laughed. "True but maybe he knows where his daughter is and most importantly how to stop her,"

"Has there been much contact between them?" Graham asked.

"None in the past three years which is when we noticed-" Bettie said as Fran coughed. "Sorry Fran noticed that is when Claire got banned from social media for inciting violence against anyone who wasn't a straight white man,"

"The thing I don't ever understand about the far-right is that some women support them when they know full well these men would love nothing more than to lock them away and just treat them as sex toys," Graham said.

"Exactly," Bettie said.

"Good afternoon," a short woman said in a very dirty apron that Graham was sure was covered in black mould.

Bettie showed the woman her Private Eye ID and passed her £20. "I would like to see the chef please and there's another £30 if you can do that for me,"

The woman shot off into the kitchen.

A moment later a very large, short and muscular middle-aged man came out in an apron that was even dirtier than the waitresses.

The man offered his hand to everyone but no one was brave enough to touch it. Graham didn't want to die this young.

"What can I do for you Miss English?" the man asked.

"Your daughter Claire Bailey, where is she?" Bettie asked.

The man pulled a chair over for himself and he sat down. "I don't know and I, I have massive concerns about my daughter and stepchildren. I gave them everything and I was never racist in front of them I promise,"

Graham wanted to call his bluff but he could see the pain in the man's eyes. He truly didn't believe in what his stepchildren and daughter did and Graham supposed the man was horrified about what had happened.

"It was their mother, a damn woman. She was *interfered* with by a black man when she was a teenager and it messed her up. I tried to make her see a therapist and I kept showing her that 99% of black people are great but she didn't believe me," the man said.

Graham felt for the man. He could feel and tell that the man truly believed he had done everything he could to support her.

Bettie leant forward. "Do you know of any way to contact her or where she might be living?"

The man shook his head.

"What about a phone call? Any strange letters? What about at Christmas?" Graham asked.

The man clicked his fingers. "My daughter hates Christmas because she believes it is wrong to get children presents and instead everyone should be giving strong straight white men presents in exchange for protection,"

Graham shook his head.

"I know, it's twisted but that works in your favour. Every year she gets me a small present because I'm a white man. I still have it and the address label is attached, do you want it?"

Graham leant forward. "Definitely,"

"I live above the café so I'll be back in a moment,"

"Thank you," Fran said as the man walked off.

Graham looked at Bettie. "I do have gloves in

the car if you want to protect yourself,"

Bettie and Fran laughed and a moment later the man returned with a small little parcel. It didn't have a return address on the label but Graham knew that the barcode and QR code on the shipping label contained tons of information about where it was printed, how it was paid for and more.

"Thank you," Graham said being brave enough to shake the man's hand as they left.

The man gently grabbed Graham's arm as he left. "I know my daughter believes in messed up stuff and she might hurt a lot of people, but please bring her back okay."

Graham nodded. "I'll try,"

But he certainly wasn't making sure promises about a woman that was threatening to obliterate Christmas for so many families and threaten the life of the nephew and his boyfriend Graham loved like his own children.

He wasn't making a single promise at all.

CHAPTER 9
22nd December 2023
London, England
16:00

When Graham had first mentioned the amazingness of London holiday traffic, Bettie had flat out believed he was joking and normally she simply would have turned on the blue flashing lights of her Federation SUV but she didn't have access to her vehicles. And the MI5 drivers were hardly going to turn on their flashing lights with the cars meant to be secret and all.

The only benefit was that it gave her time to do some more research on Claire Bailey and think up solutions to make Graham a cop once more in a fashion, but she still needed to think about the details later on.

Bettie was glad to be out of that damn traffic as she went onto the raised platform and the wonderfully soft Christmas songs playing in the background really helped Bettie to recover from how draining the traffic had been.

Parker had gone over to the main MI5 building because he had some cases to work on but Bettie was more than happy with that because it meant all these MI5 officers were now under her direct command and control.

Phryne was working with a rather cute male officer who was typing away on his computer so Bettie waved her over.

It was great seeing Phryne so excited, positive and happy to be working with her. And Bettie had a feeling she was really going to like whatever Phryne was apparently checking out.

Fran started working on the shipping label and Bettie hugged Graham quickly as he joined her.

"Something I wanted to work out," Phryne said, "was how something this massive and this kind of attack could work and who might be involved,"

Bettie nodded that was a good angle to tackle.

"So I phoned my old law professor because he specialised in prosecuting hackers. And he passed me over to his wife because she was a hacker herself and she told me there was only five hackers in the UK that could possibly pull off the attack,"

"Who?" Graham asked.

Bettie looked up at the TV screens as five pictures of women appeared from mugshots.

"These are the five best hackers in the UK that specialise in crippling European systems. Most hackers focus on UK or American systems or domestic ones. Not these three. They only focus on European systems,"

Bettie was surprised a group of people would only want to attack those ones, but everyone needed a hobby she supposed.

"Any locations?" Graham asked.

"No," Phryne said. "MI5 and GCHQ focus on them and had them under surveillance but they went missing two days ago,"

"The same exact time as Frank Clarke died," Bettie said. "It is my working theory that the Powers of Three underwent a hostile takeover two days ago that resulted in Frank's death and the new leader focusing on a plan,"

"Is our working theory that the leader is Claire Bailey?" Graham asked.

Bettie nodded. She couldn't see it being anyone else and she had contacts in other criminal organisations and they always tended to work as family run businesses. And in certain brotherhood type criminal organisations (something Bettie believed this terror group was like) no one challenged the ruling family.

Claire was the only member of the ruling family left. Bettie doubted if someone else killed Frank Clarke then the other members would have listened to them.

"What's next?" Graham asked.

Bettie took out her phone and bought up a

military file on Claire Bailey. "In the car I accessed the military intelligence database in case there was anything of use. I managed to find out that Claire served a single year in the British Armed Forces, army division, and she was fired for killing three fellow soldiers,"

"God," Graham said.

"She killed them using a single thrust of a knife in the throat and it was her signature move. Before Claire was discovered as a crazy woman she was a very valued member of the army for being ace if something went wrong,"

"Why kill her friends?" Fran asked.

Bettie really doubted Claire had any real friends but she got the question. "Because she said they were boring her and they were all women hoping to rise up through the ranks instead of accepting those positions only belonged to white men,"

Bettie hated even saying those foul disgusting words.

"So we have someone who is insane, a very skilled military-trained killer and five of the best hackers are missing. Did I get that right?" Phryne asked.

Bettie laughed. "Welcome to my world,"

"Your world's cool," Phryne said.

Bettie exchanged glances with Graham because it really was flat out weird for Phryne to be so positive towards her job. She had never ever done it before.

"I have the information from the shipping label,"

Fran said, "and this is exactly what we need to crack the case open,"

Bettie just grinned because that excited her a lot more than she ever wanted to admit.

CHAPTER 10
22nd December 2023
London, England
16:22

Graham had absolutely no idea how shipping worked, what shipping labels contained or really anything about them. He had just never needed to use them because he either went to see whoever he wanted to give something to or he just didn't send them something.

He knew this was going to be a hell of a learning experience.

Graham enjoyed the sweet Christmas songs playing in the background as Fran finished bringing up all the information from the shipping label and he hugged Bettie tight as he couldn't help but wonder how long left they really had. Especially if Claire decided to launch the attack earlier than expected.

As Frostie the Snowman started playing overhead, Graham nodded at Fran when she looked like she wanted to start.

"We analysed the information in the barcode and QR code of the shipping label," Fran said.

"And I got the guys to dust for fingerprints," Phryne said. "Claire's prints and touch DNA were the only things on the parcel besides the father's,"

Graham was glad that was exactly what they were expecting.

"The shipping parcel was shipped from canterbury high street and I've requested that they sent over their footage now," Fran said.

Graham shook his head and almost asked Fran to log into the police database on his account but he remembered he couldn't do that anymore.

"Forget about that," Bettie said, "use the Federation access to police databases to get access. If it's the shipping place I think it is then there's a traffic camera that might allow us to see inside,"

Graham nodded. She had to be thinking the label was printed at the Post Office near the top of the high street. Graham hadn't known about the traffic camera and now he seriously hoped there weren't going to be any speeding tickets coming in the next few days.

"Here," Fran said as the camera footage appeared on the TV screens and Bettie was right. Graham could see everyone at the front desk of the Post Office.

Graham looked up at the shipping label information. "The label was shipped 14:12 on the

18th,"

They all watched as Fran went through the footage to that exact time and Graham frowned when he saw a young man in a black tracksuit standing behind the desk wearing black bike gloves and then he left.

"Follow him," Graham said.

Fran used traffic cameras to follow the young man until he entered a car park and drove off on his motorbike and sadly three of the numbers were missing on the license plate.

It was even worse that there wasn't a clear shot of his face.

Graham looked at the MI5 officers eating mince pies behind their desks. "Run the first three numbers of the plate through the DVLA database and find us a match,"

All the officers got started.

And as much as Graham wanted to have a mince pie himself and feel that wonderfully buttery, sugary pastry melt in his mouth he had to find Claire Bailey.

And stop her whatever it took.

"Does the label tell us the IP address of the computer that ordered the label to be printed and shipped at the Post Office?" Graham asked.

Fran smiled. "I never said the label was printed there, did I?"

Graham forced himself not to hug Fran that was amazing news.

"The computer used to order and print the label

was using a VPN so I can't track it but I can confirm the computer was actually a laptop. An Asus to be exact with an Intel Core I7 processor and the printer was an HP Envy 4527,"

"Wow," Graham said.

Bettie nodded. "That's great but how does it help us?"

"Madam President," an officer said. "The motorbike was registered to a Mr Robert Cliffe but it was reported stolen two days later,"

"That damn... wait?" Bettie asked. "That robbery doesn't matter. This parcel was sent on the 18th that's more than two days ago,"

The officer looked a little embarrassed but Graham knew they didn't have time to watch out for people's feelings.

"What's the address of this Robert Cliffe?" Graham asked.

"I've sent it to you but the problem is, Robert is a fifty-year-old man without children,"

Graham rolled his eyes. "So whoever posted the parcel had already stolen the bike by the time of this report,"

"Because he only returned from a business trip two days ago," the officer said.

"Thank you," Bettie said.

Graham really couldn't believe how long and hard this investigation was proving to be and he hadn't met a bunch of criminals this clever for ages.

But Graham knew, truly knew that together him

and Bettie were unstoppable so the criminals would be found and he was going to make them pay.

CHAPTER 11
22nd December 2023
Rochester, England
17:30

Bettie flat out couldn't understand why idiots on the road didn't understand what a black SUV with flashing lights and sirens blaring meant. She didn't care that there was bad roadworks but the fate of Christmas for so many families rested on her.

Bettie was even more annoyed that she couldn't find a single interesting thing about Robert Cliffe that would make him involved in this crime at all, but she still wanted to talk to him.

"Thank you Mr Cliffe," Bettie said as she sat at his small wooden dining table that was wonderfully covered in a Christmas tablecloth, freshly baked mince pies and Christmas crackers.

Bettie didn't know what Christmas film was playing on the TV but it looked good and the entire small house was filled with so much cheer.

She could see that beautiful Graham and Phryne were staring at the mince pies like they were jewels or something, and Bettie had to admit they looked amazing but they had a job to do.

"You're welcome Miss English and please, call me Robert," he said. "What did you need to talk to me about at such short notice?"

"Well thank you for seeing us so quickly but, do you have any idea about who stole your motorbike?" Bettie asked.

Robert shook his head. "No I'm afraid. I'm grateful for the visitors, my poor wife is in hospital for another day or two. I hope she makes it home for Christmas,"

Bettie smiled as Robert gestured to all the family photos hanging on the walls, which was odd considering Robert wasn't meant to have any children.

"Who are all these people?" Graham asked a moment before she could.

Robert laughed. "These are my wife's kids and grandchildren. Also our foster children, we're an emergency placement for them and over time attachments happen and we were always going to foster them properly but life happened. We remain in touch thankfully,"

Bettie smiled and she was so looking forward to having her own children and family around her table at Christmas, but one of the men in the photos caught her eye.

There was a very short, slim-built young man in one of the photos so Bettie pointed to him and asked Robert who he was.

Robert smiled and frowned and then smiled again. "That's John, my wife's youngest daughter's son. A great kid if not…"

"A little racist," Bettie said not having the time to be careful.

Robert leant forward. "Please. I am the owner of a million-pound company that does deals internationally. I give all my children everything and I love them so much, the first thing I always do after a business trip is phone them and talk to each of them for at least 30 minutes,"

Bettie was about to say he was lying but she could hear the conviction in his voice and she was certain that Robert honestly tried to be the best father he could to his stepchildren and foster children.

Yet Bettie could tell by the sheer number of people in the family photos that it was a hell of a lot to call.

"My daughter said her son John fell in with a bad crowd at school but then even that crowd got scared of him when he started going about, I don't know, Power Rangers. No Power of Four."

"The Powers of Three," Bettie said.

"Yes that's the one,"

Bettie looked at Graham and Phryne. They all knew exactly how serious this was.

"Please Robert," Bettie said, "we have reason to

believe that John might be involved in a terror group that is planning a massive terror attack in three hours. We need to know where he is,"

"I don't know. My daughter texted when I was on the plane, he's gone missing,"

Bettie frowned. "Come on Robert. Where would he go? Is there a park he likes. A friend's house? Somewhere?"

Robert looked at the floor. "I do not know,"

Bettie threw her arms up in the air. She needed answers and she knew Robert was hiding something.

"John is a good kid. He doesn't deserve to suffer or get interrogated like a criminal,"

Bettie was about to snap at him when she felt Phryne hug him and then Phryne knelt down on the floor and took Robert's hand in her hers.

"I actually lost my son legally a few months ago, Sean was his name, and I was a crap mother. Very abusive and foul towards him,"

Bettie felt her stomach tighten.

Phryne smiled. "But I went to therapy, I did everything that was asked of me and I never want to be his mother again because I don't deserve that. I don't. But I want to see my son again and I want him to know that I love him *now*, I'm sorry for what I've done and I want him to know that I have changed,"

Robert nodded and Bettie forced herself not to hiss in pain as her stomach tightened more and more.

"But you see Sean and his boyfriend are flying back on a plane and if John and his friends does this terror attack then there's a chance the plane will run out of fuel before it lands and I will never… get to see, my son again,"

Robert's eyes started to wetted.

"Please Robert, if you know anything about John, please tell us. I want to see my son again and tell him that I love him,"

Robert looked up at Bettie. "He goes to the abandoned warehouses in Strood when he's upset,"

"I'll call Daniels," Bettie said.

"Don't hurt him!" Robert shouted as they left the house.

A CASE MOST CHRISTMAS

CHAPTER 12
22nd December 2023
Strood, England
17:45

Graham was amazed at how many tactical response officers from Kent Police were present as him and Bettie and Phryne pulled up outside the massive rusty warehouse that easily stretched on for tens upon tens of metres.

It didn't seem to be made up of any extra storeys but the immense metal panels missing from the metal walls allowed him to see there were tons of old machinery (probably used for making cars) still inside.

There was a large supermarket behind them with a car park where tons of people were watching them and the media was there too. Graham definitely didn't miss this about being a cop but he just wanted to get inside and find John.

"Thanks for joining us," Bettie said as Daniels in his blue business suit came over to them.

"You disappeared earlier," Graham said.

"I'm MI5 I am trained to leave without being noticed,"

Graham laughed. "What's the situation?"

Daniels frowned. "We found John inside the warehouse but he isn't coming out and we have reason to believe he's wired the entire warehouse to explode and he *is* armed with two assault rifles,"

"Bloody hell," Phryne said.

Graham looked at Bettie and she didn't look sure too. As their MI5 escort had been driving Graham had managed to look at John's social media profiles and he was a happy young man.

He had a cute girlfriend, he sadly shared the odd racist post but he had a lot of normal friends and he was doing great at school. He clearly didn't believe in The Powers of Three fully so maybe there was a chance to save him.

"Let me go in," Graham said.

He felt Bettie try to pull on his coat but he pulled away. He had to save John.

"Me too," Bettie said, "and together me and Graham can bring him out,"

Daniels looked at Phryne. "Are you joining them?"

"Hell no. I didn't pay all that money for private therapy to die a few months after,"

Graham smiled and couldn't believe that Phryne was thinking like that, but it was only because of her they had this lead so he couldn't be too harsh.

"Fine," Daniels said and Graham could hear the frustration in his voice.

Daniels clicked his fingers and a tactical response person from Kent Police passed Graham and Bettie a bullet proof vest and a military-grade helmet.

Not exactly like it would do much if John blew them up.

Then Daniels gave Bettie a warning finger. "I'm only doing this because there is no other choice and I trust you,"

Bettie smiled, she couldn't believe this was actually happening but if anything bad was going to happen then she couldn't think of a better person to have by her side than Graham.

After the tactical guys made sure they were all suited up, she kissed Graham's soft wonderful lips and everyone just looked at them as they went towards the warehouse.

Bettie had wanted to use the metal door but she knew that John had probably rigged it to explode, if that was actually true. It was weird that a young man would want to wire up a warehouse to explode.

And it didn't explain how he had gotten the explosives in the first place.

"I don't like this," Graham said as Bettie stepped through a gap in-between ripped up metal sheeting.

"I don't either but I love you," she said.

"My love ends if we die,"

Bettie looked at him and they both laughed as she knew they would love each other until the day they died, and Bettie played with the little promise ring she had on her finger. A promise that one day she actually would propose to him.

Bettie was surprised at how massive the warehouse was. It was only lit up the immensely bright lights that the police had setup outside allowing Bettie to see the thick layer of broken glass that covered the floor and the long lines of rusty machines.

"I said don't come in here," a young man said in the distance.

Bettie went towards the sound and smiled when she noticed there was a young man covered in sweat and shaking as he sat on a dirty rusty metal desk.

"Hi John," Bettie said crouching down a little so she wasn't as tall so he might not deem her as much of a threat.

"Go way or I will blow this place up,"

Bettie didn't doubt he would but she could tell he was conflicted. She had heard stories from other private eyes who worked overseas about suicide bombers and there was always that edge of determination, righteousness and a willingness to die for what they believed in.

John didn't have any of that.

"What you do here John?" Graham asked.

"Making a statement for the Powers of Three," he shouted before coughing.

"How long have you been here?" Bettie asked. "Is there someone you want me to call? Your mum,

Robert or your girlfriend,"

Bettie was surprised when John looked like he was about to cry at the mention of his girlfriend.

"She's going to hate me," John said. "I never should have done this, sent those messages and I am a failure,"

Bettie gasped when John took out a small black device that very well could have been a detonator.

"What have you done John?" Graham asked.

Bettie loved how calm he was.

"I've destroyed this place. I've sent death threats to black people. I've beat up a Jewish girl at my school just two days ago as a statement,"

Bettie took a few steps forward. "What happened two days ago?"

John smiled and Bettie was disturbed at how big his smile got, it even reached his eyes.

"The Uprising was started. Frank Clarke the idiot was killed and now the Uprising can happen and soon the world will know the Powers of Three,"

John stood up and moved his thumb over a black button.

Graham went to pull at her but Bettie moved closer to John.

"John look at me," Bettie said.

He did.

"I am a mother that wants to see my children tonight, and there are a lot of people outside this warehouse that love you, want to protect you and want to help you,"

"They can't help me. There is no going back. My girlfriend will hate me the damn Jew lover,"

Bettie smiled at John. "You haven't done anything bad yet. There is still a way back from this but if you press that button then I cannot help you,"

"She can help you with your girlfriend," Graham said.

"Really?"

Bettie smiled and nodded. "I can. I promise,"

"Liar!"

Bettie flew forward.

Tackling John to the ground.

The detonator flew across the ground.

Graham ran.

He jumped.

He caught it.

"Daniels!" Bettie shouted.

And as Daniels took John away a few moments later she couldn't help but feel scared about what would happen if John refused to talk.

He was their only lead, only hope, only chance of finding Claire Bailey.

CHAPTER 13
22nd December 2023
London, England
19:00

Bettie flat out couldn't believe the utter crap John was saying inside the small black interrogation room on the other side of the one-way mirror she was standing behind. All Bettie could do was focus on John as he started to shake, sweat and cough violently, he was clearly ill but according to Parker they didn't have time for medical attention.

And as much as Bettie hated herself, she couldn't disagree. John's medical care could wait a little longer if it meant saving the lives of thousands of people and saving even more families' Christmases, but she knew they weren't getting anywhere.

She watched Daniels and other middle-aged men in a navy blue suit interrogated John, threatened him and tried to help him out but John wasn't moving an inch towards trying to help them.

"This isn't working," Phryne said.

Bettie really wished that Graham was here but he had wanted to stay in Rochester and talk to John's girlfriend in case she could help. There were no other options and Bettie was just grateful for the extra help, but she would have loved to have spoken to him about now.

Maybe his police experience could help.

"I know," Bettie said as she looked at her sister and she felt her eyes strain in the darkness of the recording room they were in.

"Come on John," Daniels said and Bettie focused on him. "This is your final chance to help you. You aren't a bad kid, you have a bright future in front of you, don't throw this away for people that don't care about you,"

John laughed. "When the Powers of Three is unleashed and the blacks, chinks and brown people are erased from the world you will see I am not a mere mortal. I am a god that all inferiors will knee down before,"

"Jesus Christ," Bettie said as Daniels and the other officer threw their arms up in the air and left the interrogation room.

Bettie couldn't believe how twisted John was in this cult or terror group but maybe that was the way into John's mind and heart. After all she wouldn't have been surprised in over 90% of the people in EuroControl and on the planes coming into Europe were white straight men.

So surely by attacking EuroControl he was also hurting the group he claimed to protect.

Bettie wasn't sure if it would work but she was willing to try.

She was just about to go into the interrogation room when Daniels popped in shaking his head.

"The guy's nuts," Daniels said.

"True but we only have two hours left," Bettie said.

Daniels frowned. "I came in here because in a minute I am going to go and tell Parker we have nothing,"

"And then he will authorise the use of torture on a 22-year-old man," Bettie said hating that was even an option in the 21st century.

"That's why if you two have any ideas I am willing to hear them. I have no intention of torturing John but to save lives I will do it," Daniels said.

Yet Bettie hated hearing how conflicted, pained and emotional Daniels sounded, he seriously didn't want to do this.

"Give me five minutes with him," Bettie said walking out the door.

A moment later she was sitting across from John on a very warm and sweaty metal chair as John just frowned at her. Bettie smiled at him because she enjoyed how uncomfortable he was in the presence of a strong woman.

It must have been killing him inside, but Bettie hated it as the strong aroma of sweat invaded her lungs and she wanted to gag with every breath.

"John," Bettie said, "you are making a massive mistake because you claim to protect strong white men, right?"

John nodded. "Of course. That is the founding principle of the Powers of Three,"

Bettie took out her phone and bought up the employee information about EuroControl and she showed it to him.

"As you can see 94% of the people in that building are straight white men, 2% are black, 3% are Asia and 1% are Brazilian," Bettie said.

John shrugged.

"If you don't help us stop this attack then 94% of your victims will be straight white men. That isn't what you want, I thought you wanted to kill BAME people,"

Bettie forced herself not to throw up at the very things this bastard was making her say but she had to get through to him. She had to make sure Sean's plane had a safe place to land when the time came.

"She says we all need to make sacrifices in these trying times. Us lesser white man must sacrifice ourselves so the true strong white man can rise up and rule the world like nature intended," John said.

But Bettie could see he did not believe a word he was saying.

"You want to die for nothing?"

John glared at her. "I will not die. Those truly loyal to her cannot die, we are too important,"

Bettie just waved him silent, she was so done with his lies and delusions and she knew it was pointless talking to him.

"What if I told you I could find out the weakness of EuroControl and I will allow you to share it with your lot? If you simply tell me where Claire is?"

John launched himself at her.

But the chains around his ankles made him fall.

Bettie stormed out the room. John was crazy and too way gone to be of use to them.

But with less than two hours remaining until the attack was launched Bettie really didn't like their odds.

Not at all.

CHAPTER 14
22nd December
Snodland, England
19:23

"You are a very hard woman to track down Miss Hazel Robinson,"

Graham nodded his thanks for the piping hot mug of Christmas spiced coffee that Hazel's mother handed him as Hazel and him stood outside the front door so they could talk privately about John.

Graham had to admit that when he was younger Hazel would have been his type perfectly with her long blond hair, fit body and the way her pretty face lit up in the bright Christmas lights on the house was rather nice.

But she couldn't even hold up a flame to Bettie nowadays.

"What's happening with John?" Hazel asked. "Is he okay? Was he hurt?"

Graham didn't know how to say this carefully so

he just went for the truth. "John is connected to a terror group that is planning a major terror attack tonight that could threaten the world,"

Hazel frowned, but Graham couldn't understand why she wasn't surprised.

"Don't get me wrong John is a very sweet handsome boy that I really love, but he is crazy at times and even more so since he started hanging around in online forums. The Powers of Three isn't it?"

Graham nodded.

"In all honesty Detective we actually are broken up and he just cannot admit it. He's obsessed with me and he wants me to, I quote, get in the kitchen and pump out white babies for him for the race war that's coming,"

"Fucking hell," Graham said by accident but he had forgotten that he had lied to Hazel's mum about being a police detective so he could talk to the daughter.

"I know tell me about it,"

Graham really wasn't sure but he wanted to suggest something a little crazy himself. "Would you be willing to travel up to London tonight to see him? Talk to him and maybe convince him to help us,"

Hazel laughed. "Hell no. Do you know what a sexist pig he is and what he wanted to do to me without my consent? He never did it but he wants too,"

Graham couldn't even begin to imagine what he

had said to her but he just wanted to save Sean and Harry.

"Please," Graham said, "John's friends are going to launch a terror attack. I think he knows exactly where they are and we can stop this. But we need you,"

Hazel looked at the front door as her mum appeared there frowning and Graham realised she had been listening to the whole thing through the front door.

"Can I see some ID please?" her mum asked.

Graham gulped because of course he didn't have ID anymore. He wasn't a detective, he wasn't any sort of cop, he was just Graham Adams, former Kent Police detective with a beautiful sexy millionaire private eye girlfriend.

The mum grabbed her daughter and pointed a candy cane at Graham like it was a weapon.

"Mrs Robinson I can promise you I might not be a real detective but I was once and I am working with the British Private Eye Federation and MI5," Graham said sinking down to his knees.

The mum didn't look sure.

"And I am begging you to please let your daughter come up to London with me, you can come yourself and I need her help to break John,"

Hazel looked at her mother and her mother rolled her eyes.

"John knows the location of some terrorists and if this terror attack happens then there is a good chance the plane with my nephew on will run out of fuel before it's given permission to land,"

The mum frowned.

"Please help me save my nephew," Graham said.

The mother shook her head. "Fine. Are you okay with this Hazel?

Hazel looked down at Graham. "Are you sure you need me?"

"More than ever," Graham said.

As Hazel nodded Graham wanted to hug her but then he realised that the MI5 escort had taken Bettie back to London and left him behind and all the Federation vehicles were also normally in London.

There was no quick way he could get to London in time to deliver Hazel to John.

Unless he broke a very important law, he could easily impersonate a police officer and pretend that a civilian car was an unmarked police car.

He had the app on his phone from Kent Police that could show the correct light display as he zoomed through the traffic but it would be illegal.

And if he was stopped he would be arrested.

But it was a risk he was willing to take and thankfully Hazel's mum did have a Land Rover for him to use.

"Come on," Graham said. "Time's running out,"

CHAPTER 15
22nd December 2023
London, England
19:55

Bettie had left the room with the one-way mirror a few minutes ago, she seriously didn't want to listen to John hissing in pain anymore as deafening loud bass music was blasted in the interrogation room to disorientate him and he had been given a brand-new drug that made a person feel like they had been awake for days instead of mere hours.

She had no intention of learning one thing more about modern torture techniques.

Bettie sat in the middle of the raised platform just watching the bright Christmas lights sparkling, old Christmas films playing on the TV screens and Christmas carols playing softly in the background. No one else was in the room and all the MI5 officers were apparently chasing down leads elsewhere.

But Bettie knew it was truly all down to her to

find out where Claire Bailey was and it was down to Bettie to stop the attack

She just didn't know how to do it, she had tried being kind, she had tried using twisted logic and she had tried everything else she could think of.

She had failed.

Bettie really wished Sean and Harry were here along with Graham. They were a team, a brilliant one and together they were truly unstoppable and perhaps Sean (as he was the same age as John) might be able to give her some insights.

Bettie dialled Sean because she just wanted to hear his voice in the voicemail and maybe that would spark some great idea inside.

"Sean here sorry if you can't reach me at the moment. I'm probably studying, having fun or solving crime. Leave a message and I'll get back to you," the voicemail said.

Bettie forced herself not to think about what would happen if his plane wasn't allowed to land. She had been stupid and looked up plane fuel and things like that, planes never left the airport with much extra fuel because it made the plane heavier than needed.

So it would burn through more fuel anyway.

The plane might be able to circle around an airport for an hour at most if the attack happened. And Bettie knew if the attack happened it would take days for EuroControl to recover, let alone deal with the backlog.

"There's a reason why I signed over all legal stuff

to you about Sean," Phryne said as she came over to her holding two glasses of eggnog.

Bettie took it and smiled. It smelt amazing.

"Because you loved him more than I ever could." Phryne said. "You were always his mother at heart and I was just blood. I was blood that hated and took my rage and anger out on him because I was in a marriage I never wanted,"

Bettie hugged her sister as she sat down next to her. "Are you still in therapy?"

"No my therapy ended a few months back and I've finished my follow-up sessions last week," Phryne said. "But thank you for helping me realise I needed it,"

"I didn't give you much of a choice," Bettie said smiling.

"True, but I'm still grateful. My therapist helped me to realise that I was trying to catch a youth that husband John had taken from me when he wanted to get married, he got me pregnant and he left me with Sean whilst he travelled around the world doing whatever he does for the stars,"

"And I take it your therapist gave you new coping mechanisms?" Bettie asked.

"Yeah, she helped me to realise that the past is the past and I can't change it. But I can change my future and now I've worked hard to improve myself, my outlook on life and everything else. I can see myself having relationships with you, mum and Sean,"

Bettie had no idea things hadn't been right between their mum and Phryne for ages. They certainly kept that well hidden.

"But I still want you to keep Sean and be his guardian," Phryne said. "I know I love him but at the end of the day, you will always be his mother even if he isn't your direct blood. And it's fair on him that way."

Bettie hugged her sister because she really had changed. She was kind, considerate and nowadays she did actually want the best for Sean something she couldn't have cared less about for ages.

"Last concern I want to know about," Bettie said really not knowing how to phrase it. "Last Christmas you were drunk and you berated Harry and called him horrible things because he was gay and Sean's boyfriend. Before you're allowed round at Christmas I have to know. Is there a chance you would do that again?"

Phryne smiled. "Taste the eggnog,"

Bettie did and she loved the smooth creaminess and velvety softness it left in her mouth and she realised there was no alcohol in it. It still tasted amazing.

"I don't drink anymore and I still need to work on having a gay son with a boyfriend but I understand he's okay and they're a perfect couple,"

"They are," Bettie said a lot colder than she intended too but Bettie was more willing to let Phryne get into their lives if she was willing to be open-minded.

Bettie clicked her fingers.

That was it.

"You beautiful woman!" Bettie shouted hugging her sister.

"What?"

"Terrorists that are this wrapped up in ideology but also believe there is no way out. John thinks he doesn't have a family to go back to. We have to show that he does,"

Director Parker walked in with a tray of Christmas cookies.

"Parker," Bettie shouted, "I need a video call with John's mother and father immediately. And get John in here now,"

"What's going on?" Graham said with a young woman and a middle-aged one. Bettie had no idea who they were.

"We're going to convince John to give up Claire Bailey using this amazing holiday. Christmas is all about family and that is what we're going to show John,"

"Get him immediately!" Parker shouted to some officers walking in.

CHAPTER 16
22nd December 2023
London, England
20:10

Graham couldn't believe how nervous he was as him, Bettie and Phryne stood in the middle of the raised platform with John's mum and dad behind them on the TV screens on the walls.

Fran rushed in and waved at them as she stood with a whole bunch of MI5 officers who were standing at the very back of the room in case John tried anything.

Then Graham hissed as his stomach churned as John simply walked in with Daniels behind him with a gentle grip on his arm. Graham really wanted this to work because there was absolutely no other option.

He had asked Hazel to hide behind a computer desk for a moment until he said it was okay for to show herself. The last thing he wanted was for John to get overwhelmed by his parents seeing him and his girlfriend all at once.

This had to work.

"Mum? Dad?" John said. "What are these punks telling you about me?"

Graham was surprised that both John's parents looked so surprised and concerned considering that Robert had told them it was the mother that had caused all of this.

But Fran confirmed earlier that she had abandoned her sexist views a few months ago and was working hard to fight against the far-right.

"It's good to see you son," his mother said. "I'm glad you're okay,"

"Mum what's going on?" John said.

Graham stepped forward. "We wanted to show you that your parents will love you,"

John shook his head as he started coughing violently. "I don't believe you. This is a trick. *Don't trust the Government*. That's what you said Mum,"

Graham watched as his mum frowned. Graham couldn't have been surprised she was starting to regret her life choices.

"I did everything she taught me mum," John said coughing. "I made contacts, I planned what to do and we are so close to striking against the corrupt Europeans,"

"I was wrong Johnny," his mum said.

"No you weren't, "John said glaring at Graham. "You're a white man. You don't have to listen to these bitches corrupt your mind. You could have anything why won't you help me!"

Graham went straight over to him and just hugged him because John really did look like a scared little kid that was having a temper tantrum.

"It's okay John. You are safe and no one is going to hurt you. There's nothing wrong with you and I know you're a great kid deep down,"

"No one else does. Those bullies beat me up at school for being weak, those girls laughed at me when I asked out Hazel because they thought she could do better and those black boys at my schools were just dumb,"

Graham hated what he was saying but he allowed John to keep talking.

"I just, I just wanted to show the world that I am strong, I am a man and I can take whatever I want because I am a strong man,"

"The world is your oyster," Graham said, "and you can do whatever you want in the world but not like this,"

Graham broke the hug but made sure only to take a few steps away from him. "You can become a brilliant man in a high paying job and do great things but not if this attack happens,"

John looked at his parents and Graham was glad they were nodding.

"We love you son and we want you home," his parents said.

Graham enjoyed it when John's eyes went watery and wide.

"If this attack happens you will be going to prison and your life will be over. It doesn't have to be this way and you can still have a great life," Graham said.

Bettie stepped forward. "Just tell me where Claire Bailey is?"

John shook his head. "She will kill me. She hates me. She wants to kill everything,"

"Johnny?" Hazel asked and Graham subtly waved her forward as she ran over to him.

"Baby girl," John said hugging and kissing her. "I'm… I'm sorry for what I said and what I wanted to do to you. I don't know, no, I did know what I was thinking but it was the Powers of Three,"

Hazel kissed John quickly and Graham could tell her heart wasn't in it.

"We can talk later but please Johnny tell them where Claire is and then we can talk all night," Hazel said.

John looked at Graham. "Can you protect me?"

Graham nodded. "Only if we stop the attack in time,"

John sat on the floor and buried his face in his hands.

"She has a warehouse in central London, near Canary Wharf where she tapped into the superfast cables that connect London to the Continent,"

Parker and Daniels ran away and Bettie joined them.

Graham hugged him quickly. "Thank you,"

Graham rushed off after the woman he loved because there wasn't a lot of time left to save a ton of lives.

CHAPTER 17
22nd December 2023
London, England
20:55

Bettie stood outside the immense metal warehouse with sheets of silver metal welded on tight as the MI5 tactical unit prepared to breach. She was so annoyed she wasn't allowed to be part of the breacher team but she understood why.

She was useless to everyone if she died.

Bettie leant on the icy cold bonnet of a black SUV and focused on her laptop connected to the body cameras of various MI5 officers.

Director Parker stood to her left and Graham to her right and as much as Bettie would have loved to have Phryne and Fran with her this wasn't their place in the investigation and both had already done brilliantly.

A young female officer came over to them. "Heat signatures confirm there are five females in the building and another taller woman standing up,"

"That has to be Claire and the five hackers," Bettie said.

"Definitely," Graham said.

"Breach!" Parker shouted.

Bettie watched as the immense metal door shown in the body footage exploded open and MI5 officers stormed in.

They fired as soon as they saw the hackers and they zoomed towards the huge computer terminals the hackers had set up.

Within moments it was all over but Bettie didn't like this.

She ran towards the warehouse with Graham chasing after her.

A moment later she was inside and she was almost shot by the MI5 officers but she didn't care. She went deeper into the immensely cold and vast warehouse over to the computer terminals that were easily three times the height of her.

She noticed the five bodies on the ground all had Glocks in their hands so it had been self-defence, not that she was too bothered at this point.

Yet the massive ticking clock on the small laptop screen really concerned Bettie.

Graham joined her and hissed.

3 minutes to stop whatever it was counting down to.

Bullets smashed at Bettie's feet.

She leapt back.

Claire stormed towards them in a long black dress firing a Glock as she went.

The officers fired.

Claire collapsed.

Bettie charged over to her.

She kicked the gun out of her hand.

And Bettie put pressure on the gunshot wounds on Claire's stomach.

"How do I stop it Claire? Tell me," Bettie said.

Claire laughed weakly. "Don't know. All those Nazi Europeans will die today when the boiler room explodes all those scum will know English White Power,"

Bettie smashed the woman as she died. The bastard was never going to face justice but that didn't mean she was going to have a legacy.

Bettie stormed over to the computer terminals.

Two minutes left.

Bettie typed away and computer code appeared. She wasn't a hacker. She wasn't a computer expert. She wasn't anything.

That was all Sean's and Harry's department if they were here they would know exactly what to do but Bettie didn't.

She tried typing in *Kill* into the computer code but it did nothing.

She typed in *Cancel* that did nothing.

Bettie tried typing in *White Power Says No* that did nothing.

Bettie had no idea what the kill code could be for

the computer programme but she couldn't wait to find out.

Three MI5 officers came over.

Bettie grabbed a machine gun off them.

Graham did the same.

They fired into the computer terminals.

Flames erupted.

Bullets smashed into them.

Plastic shattered.

Wires were pulled out.

Computer chips smashed.

All the other MI5 officers joined in.

Within moments the computer terminals were nothing more than a flaming cracking wreck of its former self.

Bettie got out her phone and called someone anyone at EuroControl.

"EuroControl how may I help you?" a man said with a thick Belgium accent.

Bettie hung up and smiled at everyone. "EuroControl is safe!"

Everyone cheered and Bettie just hugged and kissed the wonderful man she loved because they had done it. EuroControl was safe and the terror attack was stopped.

But this wasn't over and Bettie seriously wanted to tie up all the loose ends.

CHAPTER 18
23rd December 2023
London, England
15:00

Over the next 18 hours, Graham was so happy that when Daniels had phoned him and Bettie to say that everyone in the UK and abroad who was even remotely connected to the Powers of Three had been arrested, charged and they were awaiting trial for various crimes that disturbed him a lot more than ever wanted to admit.

He was really looking forward to the Prime Minister coming into Bettie's office at the Federation's headquarters. Graham leant against the icy cold glass of the huge floor-to-ceiling window behind Bettie and Director Parker as they sat behind her immense blackwood desk that always made Graham wonder if she was a supervillain or not.

The office wasn't exactly filled with personal touches because Bettie was so rarely in here but

Graham just loved having her with him and at home.

At least the cleaners had done a great job hanging long colourful lines of red, blue and green tinsel that was so artfully combined into the breathtaking Christmas decorations that lined the white walls and immense Christmas tree tucked away to Graham's right.

It was beautiful and charming and Graham loved it because it made him know that Bettie was in charge here and she was in full command of the situation.

Which was why Bettie had demanded the Prime Minister come here for this meeting and not meet them at 10 Downing Street.

Graham still couldn't deny that Claire was batcrap crazy because Daniels had sent over the files and search history and photos from her apartment they had found a few hours later.

Graham was disgusted with how Claire had killed Frank Clarke and the other brother three days ago to siege power of the terror group and she promoted herself since her job was to recruit children and young people.

Graham had wanted to be sick everywhere when Daniels had told him that forty children had been picked up and booked into a deradicalisation programme to help combat the lies, deceit and outrageous ideas Claire had put into their minds.

And at least John had also been accepted onto a programme and with the love of his girlfriend and parents behind him, Graham had a strong feeling that he would be fine and back to normal in no time, with him only having to serve a hundred hours of community service for using the explosives that Claire had "gifted" him.

"This is a clusterfuck," the UK Prime Minister said as he came into Bettie's office.

Bettie stood up and smiled and shook the idiot's hand.

Graham hated how the man looked like a puppet in his too-tight blue business suit that highlighted his slim build a little too well, and Graham hated his Mickey Mouse ears, he was so looking forward to the Prime Minister losing his job next year.

"Why Prime Minister?" Bettie asked grinning.

"Director Parker," the Prime Minister said, "I put you in that job to get results and to follow orders. You illegally investigated this event that didn't and wasn't going to happen,"

Graham frowned and he saw in the look the two men were giving each other that something larger was happening.

"You know he needed this attack to make sure the EU listened to our demands in future," the Prime Minister said.

Graham laughed. "Wait you wanted to use this cyberattack to make a point in your political games,"

Bettie shook her head. "My fucking nephew could have died. Tons of your citizens that you are meant to protect could have died on those planes,"

The Prime Minister shrugged. "Parker still

investigated an event with political implications without my consent. He's fired. And don't get me started on you Mr Adams,"

Graham smiled.

"You impersonated a police officer and you made sure a civilian car had a flashing light. That is an offence," the Prime Minister said.

Bettie stood up. "Prime Minister, deary Prime Minister, it is Christmas and this is will be your last Christmas in Downing Street mark my words. But if you want to have a merry Christmas then just walk away,"

"Are you threatening me?"

"Of course," Graham said. "If you fire Parker and if you want the police to arrest me then me and Bettie will make your life a living hell,"

"That's my life already because of you poor people. If you want more money and if you're struggling to pay your bills, get a better job,"

Graham was so looking forward to the next election.

After a moment the Prime Minister nodded. "Because I am the best Prime Minister this country has ever had then I will allow it and I will use my brave and noble decision to use this operation in future bargains with the evil EU in future,"

As the Prime Minister left the office, Graham just shook his head. He actually couldn't believe that dickhead and judging by the look on Bettie's face she couldn't either.

"What a c-" Parker said before he realised he didn't want to say the C word in front of Bettie.

Graham laughed. "So I think that is us done then Director Parker. The UK is safe, we've in the clear for the investigation and I'm in the clear for impersonating an officer,"

Bettie gave him a mischievous grin that he had no idea what that was about but he looked forward to knowing.

"It's been an absolute pleasure Miss English," Parker said, "and you too Mr Adams. If the Federation or English family needs anything then *please* contact me,"

Bettie gave Parker a quick hug and so did Graham because Parker was just such a good man and as the three of them all left the office, Graham couldn't deny that he loved Christmas. Not only because it was such a great and magical time of year but also because it was always filled with hope, family and love.

Exactly the three reasons why he loved Christmas more than anything else in the entire world. Well maybe except the woman right next to him.

Bettie was pretty amazing after all.

CHAPTER 19
25th December 2023
Canterbury, England
20:00

After an amazing day of talking, eating and gift giving, Bettie was so grateful to be sitting on one of her large black sofas with Graham right next to her as they watched a TV special of their favourite sitcom.

Harrison and Elizabeth were sleeping leaning on their brand-new walker toys based on their favourite kid's shows, and Bettie was seriously impressed that they had only managed to tire themselves out on the walker-type toys after three hours of constant playing.

They looked so cute but Bettie couldn't deny she was sort of waiting to see how long until the walker toy moved and the kids fell onto the pillows she had placed around them. It had been an hour so far.

Bettie looked over at the other black sofa to see a very tanned Sean and Harry snoring away as they caught up on some much needed sleep. She absolutely loved having them here, she had forgotten how much fun they were, how much they made her family and just how much better her life was because they were in it.

Granted they were rubbish at taking photos and they hadn't done too much of the tourist scene because Australia was so massive and they were mainly there to see friends, but Bettie didn't mind. She would always love them.

And as Phryne snored a little too loud, woke herself up and then went back to sleep, Bettie bit her lower lip because she knew, she finally knew that after years of trouble, years of hate and years of torment from Phryne, Bettie finally had her sister back.

And she had been brilliant today with Harrison and Elizabeth, and Bettie had loved watching Phryne try to be a good person with the son and his boyfriend that she had been purposefully avoiding for ages.

And Bettie was fairly sure this was the first long, long talk they had had for ages and that really did warm Bettie's heart.

As the credits of the sitcom rolled and a jazzed up version of *Let it Snow* played, Bettie blew a kiss at Graham and she enjoyed the warming aromas of Christmas cake, brandy and mulled wine that filled the air because they still had a massive saucepan of the wine left over on the hob.

Bettie had no idea why she had bought so much wine but that was the magical thing about Christmas.

It was a time for hope, love and family but Bettie loved it because it was also a time for giving to those less fortunate and helping to make sure people had another chance.

Thankfully John and so many other children would now.

And so would Graham.

"I have another gift for you," Bettie said getting up.

"Calm down girl our family and kids are right there,"

Bettie playfully hit Graham on the head. "That special gift comes later but I spoke to the Prime Minister and the various heads of the UK Police forces yesterday,"

Graham gave her a confused look.

Bettie sat down next to him. "And there's going to be an Amendment to the Private Eye Act (2022) to create a few new legal positions within the Federation,"

Graham grinned and Bettie loved it how she could feel his excitement.

"And all UK police forces have agreed that you can still be a Detective without serving one police force in England or anywhere else in the UK. You would have to follow all the rules and regulations a police officer does with the added bonus that you can call on any police force and they have to help you,"

Graham hugged her, kissed her and Bettie screamed a little as they both fell onto the floor which made the walker toys move so Harrison and Elizabeth collapsed onto the pillows without even waking up.

"Thank you," Graham said kissing Bettie.

"Happy Christmas Graham,"

"Happy Christmas beautiful,"

And as Bettie and Graham kept kissing, hugging and rolling about on the floor, Bettie had to admit Christmas was her most favourite time of the year because it was all about love and family and it was also the time the year were really, really nice women got extra special presents from their boyfriends.

Which as Graham picked her up and carried her upstairs, Bettie was more than looking forward to that special present as their bedroom door slammed shut.

GET YOUR FREE SHORT STORY NOW!
And get signed up to Connor Whiteley's newsletter to hear about new gripping books, offers and exciting projects. (You'll never be sent spam)

https://www.subscribepage.com/wintersignup

About the author:

Connor Whiteley is the author of over 60 books in the sci-fi fantasy, nonfiction psychology and books for writer's genre and he is a Human Branding Speaker and Consultant.

He is a passionate warhammer 40,000 reader, psychology student and author.

Who narrates his own audiobooks and he hosts The Psychology World Podcast.

All whilst studying Psychology at the University of Kent, England.

Also, he was a former Explorer Scout where he gave a speech to the Maltese President in August 2018 and he attended Prince Charles' 70th Birthday Party at Buckingham Palace in May 2018.

Plus, he is a self-confessed coffee lover!

Other books by Connor Whiteley:
Bettie English Private Eye Series
A Very Private Woman
The Russian Case
A Very Urgent Matter
A Case Most Personal
Trains, Scots and Private Eyes
The Federation Protects
Cops, Robbers and Private Eyes
Just Ask Bettie English
An Inheritance To Die For
The Death of Graham Adams
Bearing Witness
The Twelve
The Wrong Body
The Assassination Of Bettie English
Wining And Dying
Eight Hours
Uniformed Cabal
A Case Most Christmas

Gay Romance Novellas
Breaking, Nursing, Repairing A Broken Heart
Jacob And Daniel
Fallen For A Lie
Spying And Weddings
Clean Break

Awakening Love
Meeting A Country Man
Loving Prime Minister
Snowed In Love
Never Been Kissed
Love Betrays You

Lord of War Origin Trilogy:
Not Scared Of The Dark
Madness
Burn Them All

The Fireheart Fantasy Series
Heart of Fire
Heart of Lies
Heart of Prophecy
Heart of Bones
Heart of Fate

City of Assassins (Urban Fantasy)
City of Death
City of Marytrs
City of Pleasure
City of Power

Agents of The Emperor
Return of The Ancient Ones
Vigilance
Angels of Fire
Kingmaker
The Eight
The Lost Generation
Hunt
Emperor's Council
Speaker of Treachery
Birth Of The Empire
Terraforma
Spaceguard

The Rising Augusta Fantasy Adventure Series
Rise To Power
Rising Walls
Rising Force
Rising Realm

Lord Of War Trilogy (Agents of The Emperor)
Not Scared Of The Dark
Madness
Burn It All Down

Miscellaneous:
RETURN
FREEDOM
SALVATION
Reflection of Mount Flame
The Masked One
The Great Deer
English Independence

OTHER SHORT STORIES BY CONNOR WHITELEY

Mystery Short Story Collections
Criminally Good Stories Volume 1: 20 Detective Mystery Short Stories
Criminally Good Stories Volume 2: 20 Private Investigator Short Stories
Criminally Good Stories Volume 3: 20 Crime Fiction Short Stories
Criminally Good Stories Volume 4: 20 Science Fiction and Fantasy Mystery Short Stories
Criminally Good Stories Volume 5: 20 Romantic Suspense Short Stories

Mystery Short Stories:
Protecting The Woman She Hated
Finding A Royal Friend

Our Woman In Paris
Corrupt Driving
A Prime Assassination
Jubilee Thief
Jubilee, Terror, Celebrations
Negative Jubilation
Ghostly Jubilation
A Spy In Rome
The 12:30 To St Pancreas
A Country In Trouble
A Smokey Way To Go
A Spicy Way To GO
A Marketing Way To Go
A Missing Way To Go
A Showering Way To Go
Poison In The Candy Cane
Kendra Detective Mystery Collection Volume 1
Kendra Detective Mystery Collection Volume 2
Mystery Short Story Collection Volume 1
Mystery Short Story Collection Volume 2
Criminal Performance
Candy Detectives
Key To Birth In The Past

A CASE MOST CHRISTMAS

All books in 'An Introductory Series':
Careers In Psychology
Psychology of Suicide
Dementia Psychology
Clinical Psychology Reflections Volume 4
Forensic Psychology of Terrorism And Hostage-Taking
Forensic Psychology of False Allegations
Year In Psychology
CBT For Anxiety
CBT For Depression
Applied Psychology
BIOLOGICAL PSYCHOLOGY 3RD EDITION
COGNITIVE PSYCHOLOGY THIRD EDITION
SOCIAL PSYCHOLOGY- 3RD EDITION
ABNORMAL PSYCHOLOGY 3RD EDITION
PSYCHOLOGY OF RELATIONSHIPS- 3RD EDITION
DEVELOPMENTAL PSYCHOLOGY 3RD EDITION
HEALTH PSYCHOLOGY
RESEARCH IN PSYCHOLOGY
A GUIDE TO MENTAL HEALTH AND TREATMENT AROUND THE WORLD-

CONNOR WHITELEY

A GLOBAL LOOK AT DEPRESSION
FORENSIC PSYCHOLOGY
THE FORENSIC PSYCHOLOGY OF THEFT, BURGLARY AND OTHER CRIMES AGAINST PROPERTY
CRIMINAL PROFILING: A FORENSIC PSYCHOLOGY GUIDE TO FBI PROFILING AND GEOGRAPHICAL AND STATISTICAL PROFILING.
CLINICAL PSYCHOLOGY
FORMULATION IN PSYCHOTHERAPY
PERSONALITY PSYCHOLOGY AND INDIVIDUAL DIFFERENCES
CLINICAL PSYCHOLOGY REFLECTIONS VOLUME 1
CLINICAL PSYCHOLOGY REFLECTIONS VOLUME 2
Clinical Psychology Reflections Volume 3
CULT PSYCHOLOGY
Police Psychology

A Psychology Student's Guide To University
How Does University Work?
A Student's Guide To University And Learning
University Mental Health and Mindset

Milton Keynes UK
Ingram Content Group UK Ltd.
UKHW020638301124
451843UK00007B/179